Peacock's Tail

by Patrick Doherty
illustrated by Stephan Daigle

HOUGHTON MIFFLIN HARCOURT
School Publishers

Printed in China

ISBN-13: 978-0-547-02710-4
ISBN-10: 0-547-02710-9

4 5 6 7 8 0940 18 17 16 15 14 13 12 11 10

Long ago, Crow and Peacock were very good friends. They looked alike, too. Both birds had plain white feathers.

One day, the friends went for a walk to look at the flowers. They liked all the pretty colors.

"Wouldn't it be nice to have colored feathers?" asked Crow.

"I know a way to change our feathers!" Peacock said. "We can paint them."

"Okay," said Crow. "I'll paint yours. Then you can paint mine."

Peacock agreed. So Crow
poured some paint out of a can
and dipped his brush in it. Crow
painted Peacock's feathers blue,
green, and black.

"Paint eyes on my tail feathers
so I can see myself," Peacock said.

So Crow painted eyes on
Peacock's tail feathers. Peacock
had never seen such a fine display
of feathers! He started to strut
around, showing off his tail.

"I am the most beautiful bird in
the world!" Peacock said.

"Now it's my turn," said Crow.
But Peacock didn't want to
paint Crow. He wanted to look at
his own beautiful tail.

So Peacock asked Crow, "Do
you like brown or black?"

"I like black," Crow said.

So Peacock picked up a can
of black paint and poured it on
Crow's head! Crow could not get
the black paint off his feathers.

Peacock left Crow standing
alone, dripping with paint. Then
Peacock took a trip around the
world to show off his feathers.

Crow stayed at home in the forest. His shiny black feathers were beautiful, but he still felt sad. Crow had lost his best friend.

Peacock showed off his feathers all over the world, but he was lonely, too. One day he went back to the forest.

Peacock found Crow in the forest. "I traveled around the world to show off my beautiful tail," Peacock said. "I have been too proud. I'm sorry."

"I missed you!" said Crow.

"I missed you, too!" cried Peacock. "When I was away, I learned an important lesson. Now I know that pride does not make you happy!"

Since that day, Crow and Peacock have been best friends.

Responding

✔ **TARGET SKILL** **Sequence of Events** What happened first in the story? What happened next? What happened last? Make a chart.

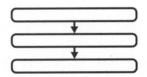

✏ **Write About It**

Text to Text Think of a different story that tells why an animal looks the way it looks. Write two sentences about the animal and why it looks that way.

WORDS TO KNOW

been	never	own
brown	off	very
know	out	

LEARN MORE WORDS

| display | strut |

TARGET SKILL Sequence of Events
Tell the order in which things happen.

TARGET STRATEGY Question
Ask questions about what you are reading.

GENRE A **folktale** is a story that is often told by people of a country.